BACK ROADS, COUNTRY TOADS

Written by **DEVIN SCILLIAN** ✳ Illustrated by **TIM BOWERS**

On a warm spring morning, Hank and Buckaroo were sitting in their favorite drainpipe near Cooper's General Store. They were licking up the last few sips of a bottle of strawberry soda and they were as happy as two country toads could be.

"I do love strawberry soda," said Hank.

"Toadally," said Buckaroo. And then they burped
"You Are My Sunshine" in two-part harmony.

Just then, eight thick rubber boots clomped out of the general store. They could hear Mr. Cooper call out, "It's going to be a beautiful day. Perfect for fly-fishing."

"Did you hear that?" gulped Hank.

"I sure did!" said Buckaroo. "It's going to be a beautiful day."

"No," said Hank. "They're going fly-fishing. FLY-fishing!"

"Whoa!" said Buckaroo. "That sounds awesome."

"We're going with them," said Hank. "But we're going to have to use our wits."

"Oh," said Buckaroo. "We better use yours, then."

"We already are," said Hank. "Come on."

The toads hopped to the gas pump and hid behind a squeegee.
They watched the fishermen loading their truck. There, between
the tackle boxes, the lid of a lunch basket was hanging wide open.

"Now!" croaked Hank.

Three country hops and KERPLOP!

They found themselves sitting between a stack of sandwiches and a bag of pork rinds. Moments later, the basket was lifted into the back of the truck. And soon, they were rolling down Highway 41.

"I smell pork rinds," said Buckaroo.

"We don't want to ruin our appetite," said Hank. "We're going fly-fishing!"

"Fly-fishing!" croaked Buckaroo. "It's going to be the greatest day of our lives!"

"Toadally," agreed Hank.

They made up a song called "When You Fish Upon a Star."
It wasn't very good, but it kept them busy until the truck pulled to
a stop near a rushing stream. Hank and Buckaroo hopped out of
the basket and over to a huckleberry bush. They thought it was the
perfect place to hide and wait, but someone else had the same idea.

"Howdy, boys," came the voice behind them. It was Emmitt the
raccoon. "You fellers are a long way from your drainpipe."

"We came with those guys," said Hank.
"They're going fly-fishing!"

"They're my favorite people," said Emmitt.
"They're here every Saturday."

"It's going to be a fly
cafeteria!" yelped Buckaroo.

"Oh yeah," said Hank. "A down-home,
big-time fly barbecue!"

Emmitt rubbed his black eyes and shook his head.
"You country toads are silly. That's not what fly-fishing is."

"Sure it is," said Hank. "It's FLY-fishing?"

"No," said Emmitt. "It's fly-FISHing. They're not fishing FOR flies. They're fishing WITH flies."

"I don't think so," said Hank. "That sounds kind of goofy."

"Look!" hollered Buckaroo. A fly was sailing through the air headed toward the stream. Buckaroo made a leap for it and sent his long tongue toward the tasty-looking fly.

"NO!" screamed Emmitt. He grabbed Buckaroo around the ankles and Buckaroo's tongue just missed the fly.

"That fly is a fake!" huffed Emmitt. "Look."

Hank and Buckaroo watched the fly land on the water. And then another. And another. And in no time, the fishermen were reeling in fish, the flies attached to their gaping fishy mouths.

"That's crazy," said Hank.

"They're just catching those smelly fish," said Buckaroo. "I don't get it."

"I happen to like smelly fish," said Emmitt. "In fact, the more smelly the better."

Emmitt darted over behind the fishermen, swiped a fish out of a bucket, and raced back to the bush with the fish wriggling in his mouth.

"See?" said Emmitt. "This is how it works."

Hank scratched his chin and Buckaroo could see he was thinking.

"Can I borrow that?" asked Hank. "Just for a second."

"Borrow my fish?" asked Emmitt. "I suppose…"

Hank dragged the fish over to a big flat rock. He laid it in the sun and then hopped back to the bush.

"What are you doing?" asked Emmitt.

"Hush," said Hank.

"Yeah, hush," said Buckaroo, though he wasn't sure what they were doing either.

Before long, a swarm of flies hovered over the fish. The swarm got bigger and bigger, and finally Hank croaked,

"Let's go fishing!"

"Yahoo!" yelled Buckaroo. Their tongues darted through the air, snapping up fly after fly, and the two toads reeled them in by the dozens.

When they couldn't possibly eat any more, they dragged the fish back to a very disgusted raccoon.

"That was nasty," said Emmitt.

"No," said Hank. "That was FLY-fishing."

Buckaroo laughed so hard that a fly flew out of his mouth.

"Look," laughed Hank. "The one that got away."

"Toadally," croaked Buckaroo.
"But we'll get him next Saturday. See you then, Emmitt."

And two very plump, very happy country toads
waddled back to town for a strawberry
soda and an afternoon nap.

To Tim who has breathed life into these toads and the rest of our menagerie.

—DS

To Caleb, Grady, and Brylie

—TB

Sleeping Bear Press®
2395 South Huron Parkway, Suite 200
Ann Arbor, MI 48104
www.sleepingbearpress.com

Printed and bound in the United States.

10 9 8 7 6 5 4 3 2 1

Library of Congress Cataloging-in-Publication Data

Names: Scillian, Devin, author. | Bowers, Tim, illustrator.
Title: Back roads, country toads / written by Devin Scillian ; illustrated by Tim Bowers.
Description: Ann Arbor, MI : Sleeping Bear Press, [2019] | Summary: "When
country toads, Hank and Buckaroo, hear some folks talking about going
'fly-fishing,' they know they have to tag along. What could be better than
fishing for flies?! So they stow away in a picnic basket and prepare for
the feast of their lives"—Provided by publisher.
Identifiers: LCCN 2019010248 | ISBN 9781534110397 (hardcover)
Subjects: | CYAC: Toads—Fiction. | Fishing—Fiction. | Humorous stories.
Classification: LCC PZ7.S41269 Bac 2019 | DDC [E]—dc23
LC record available at https://lccn.loc.gov/2019010248